GO TO MARKET

BY LORNIE LEETE-HODGE
ILLUSTRATED BY M. & G. GRAY

Published by Peter Haddock Ltd.

Half-term Holiday

One day, Mark and Mandy did not go to school. It was half-term holiday, and they would have the whole day to play, and there would be no lessons.

"What shall we do?" asked Mandy. "Let's do something exciting." Mark agreed, and they went into his home to sit down and think.

Then Mark heard his mother say that Auntie was not feeling very well and she would have to do the shopping for her. Mandy thought she could help her mother by tidying up the house. She would be very quiet so that her mother would be able to have a nice rest.

"Please, Mark," she said, "will you come and look after Debbie while I am busy?"

Mark wasn't very keen, but he said he would; Mandy found her mother's apron and tied it round her waist.

This book belongs to:

Debbie was very good, and Mark played games with her. Soon, everything was spick and span in the flat, and Mandy felt so pleased.

"It's like playing mothers and fathers, isn't it?" she asked Mark, but he didn't want to spend all his holiday looking after Debbie. He could think of better things to do!

Mandy decided she would make some coffee as her mother usually had a drink at this time. It looked easy, so she put hot water in the pot adding some spoonfuls of coffee. Soon there was a lovely smell. It was a bit difficult to pour some out without spilling but she managed it, added some sugar, and carried a cup very carefully into her mother's room. Her mother was surprised and said what a good girl Mandy had been.

"It's been fun," Mandy answered. "I pretended I was you."

The children heard a door open, and knew Mark's mother had returned with the shopping. They ran to greet her and told her all that they had been doing.

"I've made some coffee," said Mandy. "Would you like some?"

"Yes, please," answered Mark's mother and took it into her sister's room.

"I'm feeling much better now," Mandy's mother said. "I am sorry you have had to stay indoors on our half-term holiday."

"Never mind," said Mark's mother, "how would you both like to come to the market with me? You deserve a treat, you've been such good children."

There was a market held in a town a few miles away, and they could catch a bus to it.

"Yes, let's go now," they both cried.

Mandy's mother said she felt quite well again, and Debbie could stay with her. Off they started, but were too late for the bus; it had just left when they reached the bus stop. "Never mind," said Mark's mother, "it isn't far, we'll walk."

But Mark and Mandy were delighted when a friend came by in her car, and stopped. "Would you like a lift?" she asked, and they all climbed into her car.
"This is better than the bus," Mark said.

The two ladies talked, while Mark and Mandy amused themselves by counting the different cars which whizzed past them.

They soon reached the market, passing the bus on the way and giving a friendly hoot as they swept by.

At the Market

The children had not been to a market before, and were excited when they reached the crowded square where it was held. There were lots of stalls with goods to buy on them. "Don't go too far away from me," Mark's mother said, "or you might get lost."

Mark and Mandy rushed from side to side. "It's much nicer than shops," Mandy thought, "and more fun to buy in the open air."

Some of the stalls had gay coverings above them to protect the goods from the hot sun, or the rain if a shower came. The stall owners stood at the side calling out the special bargains they were selling. In another part there was the cattle market where animals were sold, but they did not go to see this; they liked this part much better.

"Come along, there's lots to see," Mark's mother reminded them. And they had yet to spend their pocket money.

Mark and Mandy wandered around trying to decide what nice thing they would buy.

Then Mandy saw a flower stall with some lovely big blooms for sale and thought she would take a big bunch home for her mother, but Auntie told her to buy them later, or they would fade before they reached home.

"Now I must do some shopping," she said, and took a list from her handbag. "I want to buy some fruit first, so we will go to the stall over there."

There was a big pile of lovely red apples on it. "Those will be just right, I think," she said.

She asked the man the price, and he filled a bag of them for her. Then she found she had left her basket at home. The apples would be heavy to carry so the man said he would keep them for her if she came back for them.

"I think we had better buy another basket to put the different things in, it will be awkward to carry them in odd bags," Mark's mother said. She was sorry she had forgotten to bring one. "Come along, children, we'll go and see what we can find."

Another stall was selling baskets and bags, and amongst them, was a small checked bag on wheels which could be pulled or pushed along. "Let's have that one," cried Mark, "it will be better than a basket."

So his mother bought it and the apples were put into it. Mark pushed the trolley bag.

An old man was standing by another stall, and the stallholder was shouting, "Lovely ripe bananas." He was buying a large bunch while his dog sat beside him. Mark wanted to pat the dog, but it growled and wasn't friendly, so his mother hurried on to another stall.

There was another fruit stall with boxes of shiny apples and juicy pears. The man was shouting, "Ripe apples and pears," and seeing Mandy and Mark, he gave them a ripe pear each. "Thank you very much," they said.

The pears were very juicy, and their faces were soon sticky, but they enjoyed them. He was a smiling man, and lots of people were buying his fruit. Mark's mother bought some more apples and some pears, and he put them carefully in the new bag.

"We have enough fruit," she said, "I want to buy some fish now," so they left this part of the market.

The Fishmarket

They then went across the square to the fish-
market. "Oh, it smells," Mark said, but they
soon forgot this when they saw the stalls filled
with different fish. There was a big pile of
blue-grey mackerel, and the man was shouting, "fresh today, just out of the sea." Next to
him was another stall with eels and plaice on
it.

Auntie did not stop here, but went on to a
particular stall. Behind it was a big, jolly man
dressed in a seaman's jersey and a yachting
cap. His arms were tattooed. He knew Mark's
mother, and to tease the children, held up a
huge squid with long squiggly arms and a
round head with eyes that stared at you. Mandy was scared and hid behind Mark, but he
was brave and wanted his mother to buy this
strange fish. But she preferred to have some
fresh haddock!

Moving around the market, they came to Pets' Corner and here there were animals and pets of all kinds. Cats and kittens, puppies, big and little dogs, rabbits, hamsters and even hens, chickens and ducks. Mark and Mandy stayed a long time watching some puppies playing in their cage. They were so nice.

"Wouldn't it be lovely to have a puppy?" Mandy asked Mark. "I think that little brown one is sweet." Mark liked a black one. But Mandy knew she wouldn't be able to keep a puppy in their flat. Mark wanted to buy a big, fat rabbit until his mother reminded him that his cat, Smudge, would not like a playmate as big as himself.

It was rather noisy in this part of the market,

the dogs barking and the hens and chickens making a din, but the children enjoyed being surrounded by so many different kinds of animals.

"Well, children," Mark's mother said, "we have been here a long time, but we really must go on now."

Mark and Mandy hated to leave Pets' Corner, but Mark's mother promised to buy them an ice cream as

they were feeling hot. Further along the square, they saw an old-fashioned ice cream stall gaily painted and with a striped awning above it. The ice cream man was also jolly, and had a bell hanging beside his stall which he rang loudly at times to let people know where his stall was. He sold lovely wafer and cornet ices, and the children stood for a few minutes deciding which they would have. In the end, Mandy had a cornet, but Mark chose a wafer. He soon ate his and, of course, wanted another!

"You musn't be greedy, Mark," said his Mummy, "one is quite enough for the moment. Perhaps later."

So Much to See

Mandy had quite a fright as she and Mark wandered among the stalls. Suddenly an old man, scissors in his hand, popped his bald head out from behind some coats hanging up, and called out, "Cheap materials, all good quality."

Mark's mother stopped to look at his rolls of material as they were very attractive. She wanted to make a dress for herself, and also some trousers for Mark. The old man showed her one roll of cloth after another, and at last she chose the two she wanted. When the material was wrapped, his mother decided to carry it as the parcel would get very crumpled in the trolley bag.

Mandy felt a little envious and wished her mother had come with them, then she might have had material for a new dress.

While his mother went to look at another stall, Mark and Mandy walked on through the market. There were such a lot of interesting things to see, and they hoped they would be able to come again another day. Hanging up above one stall, Mark saw some brightly-coloured plastic fishes tied on long strings which swayed in the breeze. They looked great and he knew he wanted one more than anything else in the world; he could put it in his bath or it could hang in the open window of his bedroom and he could watch it swaying in the wind. He asked the man how much and then ran to find his mother who was carrying his pocket money in her handbag. He was very disappointed when his mother would not let him buy it. She told him it was a waste, and he should keep his money for something better.

"Well, it is a bit babyish for you," commented Mandy, "babies have toys to float in their baths."

Mark felt rather awkward when he remembered this, and did not say any more. Perhaps he would see a fine boat.

In another corner, out of the sun, the children saw some huge tanks full of fish. There were goldfish and tropical fish of many different kinds, and lots of people were standing round the tanks watching them. Mark and Mandy joined them, and were fascinated when the stallkeeper told them that some were "man eaters" and would bite your finger off if you put it in the water. Everyone laughed, but Mandy thought it might be true so she kept her hand safely behind her.

A boy came and bought a fish. The stallkeeper tried to catch it with a net. "No, that's not the one I want," cried the boy, "it's that one." The other fish were scurrying about in the water, and at last, the man caught the right one. He put it in a bag full of water, but the boy still thought he had been given the wrong one.

"I'd love to have a proper aquarium," thought Mark, "with lots and lots of fish."

Mark watched enviously as the boy carried the fish away. Perhaps his mother would let him buy a real fish this time.

Just then his mother came along and Mark rushed to ask her for some money. This time she told him his cat, Smudge, would only catch the fish if he bought one, so that once more he was disappointed. It did not seem that he would be able to buy anything that day! "Grown-ups always have a reason to up-set your plans," he thought.

The Antique Market

"This is the most exciting part of the market," said Mark's mother, as they crossed the road. "It's full of old things, and sometimes you can find wonderful bargains if you look hard."

There were several stalls covered with a mass of things, from books, gramophones, lamps, ornaments and candlesticks. There was even an old kettle amongst them. People were turning the goods over and arguing about the prices. A splendid trumpet caught Mark's eye but he decided his Mummy would not let him buy it, even if he had enough money!

Mandy and Mark started to poke among the books, so his mother said, "I'll take the trolley bag now, you might lose it here, and then we won't have anything for supper."

After a while they moved away from this fascinating stall, and Mandy and Mark had still not spent their pocket money.

Outside his shop, one store-keeper had a small stall, but he invited everyone to come inside where he had many things on view. It was a bit dark inside after the sunlight when Mandy and Mark went into the shop. They found many strange articles as well as antique furniture. Mandy found a gold rimmed mirror propped up against the wall, and had a lovely time making faces at herself in it, then preening this way and that, just like her mother. Mark came to her, and they giggled and laughed at the strange faces they made in another mirror which distorted the image.

Mark found an old engine with one wheel missing, so he put it back. He wondered whether the train had belonged to a little boy many years before, and if he had broken the wheel.

His mother was talking to the shopkeeper about some old chairs. She was interested in old furniture. There was so much to see in a shop like this, and Mark and Mandy thoroughly enjoyed looking at everything.

The back room at this shop held even more

treasures. An old-fashioned bird-cage stood on a green chest with a knob missing, and a broken telescope lay on the floor. Mark and Mandy found two big chairs with stiff backs covered in pretty material. They sat in them, but the seats were so high that their feet did not reach the ground. On the top of an old cupboard stood a blue bowl. It was rather large, and Mark wondered what it had been used for, — it would hold such a lot of soup!!

"Does the man dust all the things in this room?" asked Mandy.

"It must take him a very long time." Mark's mother said she did not know, but she expected the rooms were cleaned regularly.

"I wouldn't like to have to do it," said Mandy.

"We must see the doll's house before we go," said her Auntie, "it's over here."

In a corner, against the wall, was an old doll's house. The side had been taken off to show the contents, and Mark and Mandy knelt down on the floor to see what was inside. On the ground floor was the dining room with old fashioned chairs, a shiny table and a sideboard. A picture hung on the wall. Next was a kitchen with pots and pans and huge jars. Upstairs, there was a funny bathroom with a high sided bath and taps above it. The bedroom was very grand with a brass bedstead and a table beside it with a lamp on it.

"Oh, isn't it lovely?" cried Mandy. "Look, there are even two pictures on the wall. Do you think I could buy it?"

Her Auntie told her it was too expensive. "It's an antique," said the shopman, and Mandy knew this meant it was very old and very valuable.

Time for a Rest

It grew very hot in the market during the afternoon. The sun shone fiercely, and the air seemed heavy. Mark's mother looked at the children, and could see they were getting tired, – in fact, she was beginning to want a rest herself. Then she had an idea.

"Shall we go and sit by the river for a while?" she asked them. "I've finished my shopping, and we shall have time before we go home." Mark and Mandy thought it would be wonderful. A friendly shopkeeper promised to keep the trolley bag for them with all the parcels in it until it was time for them to catch the bus home. So they left the market, and walked along the road until they came to a sign saying "To the River," they went down a path and there was the river, so cool and beautiful.

"Let's go over there under the trees," said Mark. It was shady there, and the three of them sat down on the grass to get cool. It was lovely just to sit and look at the river flowing past them.

They sat for a while enjoying the river and watched the gulls swooping backwards and forwards, sometimes coming to rest on the water.

"I wish I could fly," thought Mark.

Mark and Mandy soon felt cooler, and as there was a café overlooking the river, they decided to go there and have some tea or lemonade to drink. It was not crowded and they soon found an empty table. A friendly waiter came along for their order and Mark's mother ordered a pot of tea for herself and long, cooling drinks for Mandy and Mark.

When it was brought, Mark was disappointed not to see a straw in his glass; he loved drinking through a straw, but still, the waiter had put ice cubes in the lemonade. This made it beautifully cold, and it was fun to see the lumps at the bottom of the glass when he had drunk the last drop of lemonade, and to turn these over and over in his mouth. They were only thirsty, and did not want anything to eat when the waiter asked if they needed any cakes. "I don't think I would like to be a waiter," said Mandy, "even in a café by the river. I expect he gets very tired sometimes."

"I'm sure he does," agreed her Auntie, "but this waiter looks very cheerful and smiling."

It was pleasant sitting in the shade watching the river. Some boats passed, and Mandy and Mark waved to the people in them. Then they saw something different coming along. "What's that boat, Mummy?" asked Mark. "I haven't seen one like it before."

There was a red flag on it, and Mark wanted to see it closer. His mother explained that it was a barge and that it would stop at the toll bridge a little way further on.

"Do let's go and see," he begged as he finished his drink.

As they hurried along the path they seemed to be racing the barge, but they got to the toll

bridge just in time. As the barge came nearer to the bridge, out came the toll bridge keeper. He looked very important in a blue uniform and a peaked cap. The children watched eagerly as he leaned over the railing and held out a box on a long pole. The man on the barge called out a greeting to him, and dropped some coins in the box.

"Why is he doing that?" asked Mandy.

"That is the payment for using the toll bridge," Auntie answered.

The bridge keeper had a small dog which barked loudly at the cat which he could see on board the barge.

Something funny

They returned to the market and Mark and Mandy were pleased they had seen something new — a barge and the way tolls were collected on the bridge. As they drew nearer the stalls, they could hear a man shouting, "this perfume will make you smell like Liz Taylor." A fat lady in the crowd laughed, and the man went on, "if you wear it, you'll be wonderful." He had little sprays of different perfumes which he squeezed and tiny jets shot out over the crowd. Mandy did not like the smell of them and, of course, Mark thought they were silly, so they did not wait any longer, and left the man still trying very hard to sell his goods.

"I thought we had seen all the market," Mandy said.

"No," replied Auntie, "there's lots of stalls you haven't seen yet."

Mark suddenly saw a school friend and went to join him. "You stay with me, Mandy," said her Auntie, "the two boys can amuse themselves."

Mark saw an old clothes stall, and, with his friend, went to it. They began trying on some of the things displayed there. Mark put on a very grand coat with braiding on the shoulders and shiny brass buttons. The material had once been a bright green, but oh! dear, it had faded.

"I'm sure this was a general's coat," said Mark, and his friend, Paul, then found a red coat with braid across the front. He put it on, and they did laugh when they saw themselves

 in a mirror. Mark's would have fitted a giant, Paul thought, and Paul really looked strange in a soldier's coat and his school cap on his head. The trousers were far too long, and the stall-keeper shouted to them not to get them dirty on the ground, so they tried on different old hats. There were army hats with shabby feathers (these must have belonged to generals) and

small red caps worn in Africa as well as big sun helmets which covered their faces completely. What fun!

Mandy had found a stall covered with old pictures, and she began turning them over. Some of them were old and dirty, some had broken frames or were torn, but then she saw a picture she liked. It was in a frame, and the glass wasn't broken. It showed a family of long ago, with ladies dressed in long dresses and hair piled high on their heads, sitting in a garden. She propped it up against some others, and thought how pretty it was. Perhaps she would be able to buy it. Mark had left his friend, and came along to join her.

She showed him the picture, but he didn't think much of it; he still wanted a fish. Auntie was talking to someone so Mandy had to wait for a little while before she could ask her. She felt she wanted it more than anything else.

Soon Auntie came along, and Mandy showed her the picture, and said how much she wanted it. Auntie also thought it was very pretty, and said she would buy it for her as a present; Also, she said if Mark really wanted a toy fish, he could have one.

The man wrapped the picture very carefully in brown paper, and Mandy threw her arms round her Auntie's neck and kissed her. She was so pleased with her present.

"Oh, thank you Auntie, it will look lovely in my bedroom. I shall look at it every day."

Auntie laughed. "I expect you won't even notice it after a few weeks," she teased.

Mark, too was glad he could have the fish, and ran off to buy it.

He took great care to choose one which was the right colour.

This was a shiny red fish, right on the top, and the man had to take them all down to un-hook it for him.

"Mind you don't lose it," he said, but Mark carried the parcel very carefully.

Goodbye to the Market

Mark and Mandy were beginning to get tired of the market now, it seemed hot, noisy and smelly to them, and they were ready to go home. Mark's mother told them she only wanted to buy some cheese which she had forgotten, and then they would go to the bus stop.

Mark and Mandy decided to have one last look at the stalls, and set off to find Pets' Corner first. The rabbits and the other small animals were still there, but some of the puppies had been sold. Mandy hoped those which had been left were not missing their brothers and sisters, but they seemed playful, and so did the kittens in the next cage, — perhaps it was all right.

"Come along," ordered Mark, as Mandy was making a hole in the paper wrapping and having another look at her picture.

"Mind you don't drop it. Let's go to the antique shop again, and then find Mother at the cheese stall."

The man at the antique shop let them have another look at the doll's house; there were other children around it so Mark and Mandy did not stay. As they passed the fishmonger with the tattooed arms, he called to them, "Something nice for you," and he gave them each a lovely fruit lolly. It was so cool and refreshing.

"Isn't he a nice man," whispered Mandy, "but I didn't like his squiggly fish. It was horrid."

"It wouldn't hurt you," laughed Mark.

They thanked him, and went on to find Mark's mother looking at a huge display of cheeses, the biggest Mandy had ever seen. The man selling cheese had just cut a large piece and was weighing it on the scales. It was just right, so he wrapped it up and Mandy put it in the trolley bag. There were many different kinds of cheese, and Mark wondered why some of them had little holes in them. This was a special kind, the man told him, and gave both children a tiny piece to taste. They didn't like it very much, but were too polite to say so.

Mandy remembered the flowers for her mother, and they went back to the flower stall. Many of the flowers had been sold, but there was still a lovely perfume surrounding it, and it was much nicer than the smell of cheese or fish. Her Auntie helped her to choose a special bunch of flowers, and said she would carry them for her as they would get crushed in the trolley bag.

"Mummy will like these," thought Mandy.

Off they went to the bus stop. Mark and Mandy were tired and glad to be going home. They had had a lovely day, and were yet to have another adventure before they got out of the bus. "Isn't it lucky we bought the trolley bag?" asked Mark who felt he had chosen it. "The shopping would be awfully heavy to carry in a basket." His mother agreed, and said it was a good buy and would be useful when she went shopping at home.

A Bus Ride

There was quite a queue of people waiting at the bus stop, and they could hear the bus coming round the corner.

"Hurry, children," said Mark's mother, "we don't want to miss it again; we should have to walk home. There might not be a kind friend to give us a lift in her car this time."

She took some money out of her purse as they took their places in the queue. It was always so difficult finding change when you were crowded by other passengers.

"What a pity it isn't a Red Arrow bus," said Mark, as he liked pushing through the turnstile.

"Hold your picture tightly, Mandy," and she clutched it with both hands, and Mark held his parcel carefully. He was longing to get home and float his fish in the bath. He hoped they would soon be home.

The bus came along, turned round, and opened its doors to let the passengers get out. Then the people waiting in the queue jostled and pushed to climb aboard. There were so many wanting to get on, that Mark and Mandy were afraid they would be left behind. Mark jumped on, and his parcel nearly fell out of his hand. "Come along, hurry it up," called the conductor, and somehow everyone got on.

Mandy and Mark and his mother were almost last. They held on tightly as with a great lurch the bus started and moved off down the road. A kind gentleman gave Mark's mother his seat, but Mark and Mandy had to stand close to the conductor. "Oh, dear," moaned Mandy, "it is crowded."

She held her precious picture close to her. She wished the bus had more seats, but Mark (who knew everything) said it was often, "Standing room only" in crowded buses, and at any rate, it was better than walking all the way home. Mandy privately thought it was difficult to stand when the bus swayed! And it was so hot!

The other standing passengers near the children let them squeeze through to stand near the window. Then they could see everything, and it was exciting. Suddenly, as the bus turned a corner the driver jammed on his brakes, and everyone was jerked forward. "What is it, what's happened?" they asked.

Right in front was a red car, but it wouldn't start. The driver of it looked embarrassed, and was trying very hard to make it go, but try as he would, nothing happened. The bus driver had managed to stop his bus a few yards away from the car, and he now blew his horn loudly.

His passengers were getting impatient, and all seemed to talk at once. The bus driver had been clever to stop the bus in time to avoid crashing into the car which was blocking the road.

At last, the motorist climbed out of his red car and came to speak to the bus driver. "I'm very sorry," he said, "the car is new, I'm not used to it and am not sure how to start it."

Mark said, "There's another queue now but this time it's behind a bus, not waiting for it."

At last, passers-by helped the driver and between them they managed to push the car to the side of the road, out of the way of the bus. The road was clear again, and the bus could go on.

"Try switching the engine on," called out the driver as, with a toot on his horn, he drove the bus away. The passengers watched as the car driver seemed to be doing this. This time, the engine roared into life, and he was soon driving down the road. How silly he must have felt not to have thought of this before.

Home Again

At last the bus stopped near their home, and Mandy, Mark and his mother climbed out.

"What a journey," they all exclaimed as they went up the stairs to Mandy's flat. Debbie and her mother were so pleased to see them, and Mandy gave them the presents they had bought in the market.

Mandy and Mark tried to tell them all the adventures they had had, at the same time, so her mother said, "Wait until you have had some tea, it's all ready for you."

Mark's mother told her about the delay caused by the red car, and Auntie laughed and said, "Poor man, how awful for him."

Mandy was impatient to hang her picture up at once in her bedroom, but her mother said her father would do it when he came home. "I wish he would hurry up," she said.

For once in his life, Mark longed for bedtime. He was ready to go as soon as he had finished his tea, for he was tired. He wanted to play with his new fish, too. He didn't mind if Mandy did think it was babyish.

At last it was bath time, and he had great fun making the fish jump and dive in and out of the water just like a real one. Then he carefully dried it, and hung it on a string near the window. As he lay in bed he could watch it blowing in the breeze through the open window and thought how pretty it looked.

Lying in bed, his mind was full of the wonderful half-term holiday treat. . . of how funny he and Paul had looked in those old clothes at the market, then there was the barge on the river and, finally, the exciting adventure on the bus home.

"What a day," he thought, as he fell fast asleep.

When her Daddy came home that night, Mandy told him all about her happy day at the market, and the wonderful picture she had. He promised to hang it for her, and after his supper he brought a hammer and nail and put it just where she could lie in bed and look at it. She was so pleased, she didn't want the light out. So her mother left a night light burning and Mandy was able to look at it until she went to sleep. She lay and imagined the people in the picture came alive and stepped out of the frame to talk to her.

She soon fell asleep and dreamed that they were all playing together in the lovely garden of the picture. What a surprise to wake up next morning and find she was still in her own bed, and the picture on the wall for her to see. What a pity she could not take it to school to show to the other children, but it was a bit too large for that.

She and Mark had had such a super day at the market that already she was thinking of how quickly they might go again. Perhaps her Mummy would take them next time and then she would be able to show Debbie all the colourful shops and stalls. She hoped it would be soon.